The Ballad of Limpy Blindy

by
Duncan Kennedy & Ishbel Borland
Illustrated by Greer Norquoy

© Illustrations and cover design
by Greer Norquoy

Printed and Published by The Orcadian Limited,
Hell's Half Acre,
Hatston,
Kirkwall,
Orkney

ISBN 1 902957 04 0

Introduction

Limpy Blindy is nothing short of a wee miracle.

The first days of a lamb's life on the hill in the remote north isles of Orkney are filled with danger.

Papa Westray weather at lambing time can, in a matter of minutes, turn dangerously wintry, with chilling showers sweeping in over Tirlo and down the hill to the loch. Lambs huddle behind their mother to avoid a soaking.

However, in the air there is another menace – The Backies. The greater Black-Backed gulls, huge, sinister birds who sweep across the fields searching for a weak lamb or one separated from its mother. They are merciless.

It was to one of these scavengers that Limpy Blindy fell victim. In the attack he lost an eye and was lifted high into the air before being dropped from a height, probably during a squabble between the birds over their prey.

The farmers shook their heads when Katy carried the little bundle back to School Place 'It'll never make it . . . one eye gone, the back shattered in the fall . . . it'll never make it.'

But they hadn't reckoned with the will to survive of the lamb and the concern and determination of Katy. Patiently she nursed the broken little bundle and every day saw little improvement. When the lamb, comfortable in his straw-lined cardboard box, took his first sook on the bottle, the cheers from School Place could be heard around Papa Westray.

Every day he grew a little stronger. Katy crept through during the night to check progress. Soon, miraculously, the lamb, now named, inevitably, Limpy Blindy was chasing around the field in front of the house with the other caddie-lambs. The fastest three legs on Papa Westray. Our own little miracle.

Katy

Today on the hill above the loch Limpy Blindy grazes contentedly with the other sheep, turning his head lopsidedly to gaze at passers-by through his one good eye and hopping after the rest of the flock as they move among the pastures.

As for Katy she is now a third year student at Glasgow University Veterinary School. How big a part did Limpy Blindy play in Katy's decision to follow a career in animal care? Only an island girl and her wee miracle know that.

Jim Hewitson
OCTOBER 1999

The Ballad of Limpy Blindy

If you look at a map you will see far up at the top of Scotland, some islands called the Orkney Islands. One of these islands, a very small one very far away, has a farm on it. On the farm lives the farmer, the farmer's wife, the farmer's daughter and lots of animals.

There are cows and hens, one very old pig called Mrs. Porker and lots of sheep. There are also lots of rabbits but the farmer doesn't like them as he thinks they are very greedy and eat up too much grass.

The farmer's dog Jess, who is a sheepdog, likes to chase the rabbits sometimes, but never actually catches any. This is a good thing for the rabbits of course who are all very fond of Jess and enjoy a good chase now and again.

One day at lambing time the farmer and Jess the sheepdog were in the fields to check on the new-born lambs. There were a lot of new lambs and the farmer was very pleased.

Suddenly Jess gave a funny bark and the farmer went to see what was the matter. To his surprise he saw that Jess had found another new-born lamb. It was all on its own. It's mother was nowhere in sight.

The farmer was sad as he knew that young lambs with no mother to look after them often do not live. When he looked at the lamb he was even more sad for he saw that it was a very tiny lamb. It had only three legs and a little stump, instead of four strong legs, and it also had only one good eye.

However, when the farmer picked up the lamb, it said "BAA-GH" very loudly and kicked strongly until he put it down again. What a brave little man you are," said the farmer. "I think you deserve a chance." He put the lamb inside his overalls and took it up to the farmhouse.

At the farmhouse he showed the lamb to his wife and daughter and his daughter just loved the tiny creature. "Don't worry, dad," she said. "I'll look after the poor wee thing."

She did, too. She looked after it so well that in no time at all it was ready to join the other lambs in the field.

Before it did, however, the farmer came in one day with something he had been working on in his shed. "This is for the wee lamb," he said to his daughter and put a round wooden thing on the table.

"Why, dad, it's a wooden leg! That was very nice of you." Just then the farmer's wife came in. "Here's a little thing I've been sewing for the lamb," she laughed and laid beside the wooden leg a little black eyepatch.

So he made him a patch and a wood-en leg so he could get a - round,

Well, the farmer's daughter was very pleased indeed. She strapped the wooden leg on the lamb at once and, once he got used to it, the little lamb was also very pleased. He wasn't so taken with the eyepatch, which after all only covered up his bad eye and didn't help him to see any better. He was a kindly little soul, though, and as his mistress liked it he wore it gladly.

The little three-legged, one-eyed lamb was soon running and leaping around the fields just like all the other lambs. In spite of having a wooden leg he was mostly able to keep up with the rest and joined in every single one of the silly jumping competitions. He actually won sometimes!

There was one thing which troubled him. As anybody knows, who has lived on or been to a farm, every time it rains there is a lot of mud about. By the time all the animals have been walking through the mud it can get very deep and sticky - the sort of mud which can pull your wellington boot right off your foot if you're not careful.

Sometimes, when there was sticky mud about, the poor lamb's wooden leg would get stuck fast. Often he could not pull it out and would have to take it off and leave it for the farmer to pull out for him.

When this happened the other animals would gather round and make fun of him, calling him names. (Animals can be cruel, just as children are who call people names) The animals would chant to a little tune which they had made up :- "LIMPY BLINDY, wooden leg can hardly see, LIMPY BLINDY, wooden leg can hardly see." This is how our little lamb came to be called "Limpy Blindy".

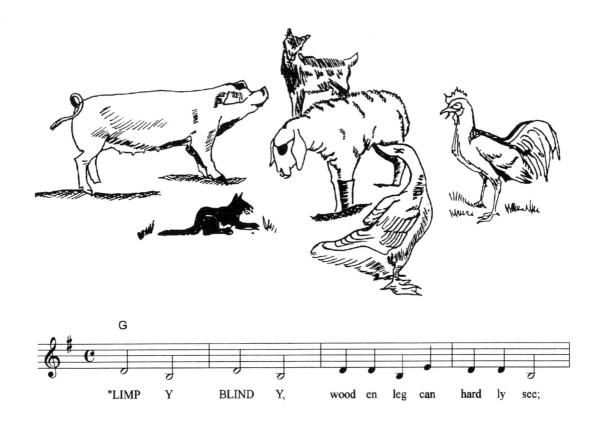

Although he was hurt by all this teasing and name-calling, Limpy Blindy was brave and would never cry. He never tried to get his own back on any of the animals as he was too nice to call people names or to try to make a fool of them. He knew that the other animals didn't really think that they were hurting him.

Then one hot, stuffy day there was a terrible thunderstorm. It didn't rain but it was very hot and there were a great deal of very loud roars and rumbles of thunder. Soon these came nearer. Then there were very sharp and bright crackling strokes of lightning, almost as if giants in the sky were taking photos with huge camera flashes.

The animals were all very frightened and ran into the big hay barn. The farmer then shut the door of the barn, thinking that the animals would all be safe inside during the storm.

The storm got worse and worse. The thunder was very very loud, right above the farm. The lightning flashes were coming faster and faster. As if this wasn't bad enough, the wind blew stronger and stronger. It made a horrible moaning, whistling sound as it blew over the barn.

there was a dread-ful thun-der-storm which - no - one will for - get.

Then suddenly there was the loudest bang yet and a very bright flash . The animals, peeping out, saw that there had been a lightning strike right beside the barn and that the dry grass had caught fire.

The animals were terrified. They knew that if the fire reached the wooden barn, which had a lot of hay in it, they would probably all be killed.

As they watched, the strong wind blew on the fire and they saw the flames sprouting and smelled the smoke. Some of the younger animals began to cry and even the older animals began to bellow and bleat with fright. Only Mrs. Porker the pig, who didn't really know what was going on, wasn't terrified.

Just outside the doors of the barn was a big wooden barrel with a spout at the bottom. This barrel was full of water and when the farmer washed the floor of the barn he used to turn the spout and let the water flood out. Limpy Blindy had seen the farmer do this several times.

But some-one's squeez-ing be-neath the door, good job he's ve-ry small.

Without saying a word to anyone, Limpy Blindy began to squeeze under the doors of the barn. Luckily he was very small and there was a dip in the floor just where the doors met. After a lot of squeezing and pushing he just managed to get out beneath the barn doors.

Once he got out Limpy ran up to the big water barrel. He hit the water spout a mighty kick with his wooden leg. Thank goodness it *was* a wooden leg, as he would probably have hurt himself quite a lot by giving such a powerful kick with his *real* leg. His kick did the job first time, and just in time, for by now the flames were beginning to lick about the barn walls.

When Limpy Blindy kicked the water spout it broke off and all the water in the barrel rushed out onto the ground. There was a lot of water and poor Limpy Blindy got very wet indeed.

He hit the spout a might-y clout, the spout fell off, the wat-er rushed out.

The water flooded over to where the grass was on fire and, with a mighty HISSSSS-ING sound, the fire went out. There was still plenty of smoke and steam but the fire was OUT and all the animals were saved.

Just then the farmer came. He had heard all the noise the animals were making and thought that they were just frightened of the storm. He saw what Limpy Blindy had done and he knew that if it hadn't been for the brave little lamb he would have lost his barn and all the animals in it. (And also rather a lot of hay, which isn't cheap!) The farmer was very pleased.

The storm suddenly stopped and all was quiet.

When the farmer let the rest of the animals out of the barn each one, from the big cows down to the newest lambs, went up to Limpy Blindy. Every single one said "Thank you very much for saving me. I'll never call you LIMPY BLINDY again. You are very brave and clever."

"LIMP-Y BLIND-Y thank you for sav-ing me. LIMP-Y BLINDY, you'll go down in Histor-y."

Limpy Blindy replied, "You are very welcome. I am glad I was able to help, but please don't stop calling me LIMPY BLINDY. After all, this is now my name."

Nowadays when Limpy Blindy goes about the farm, the other animals bow to him. They still chant their little tune but the words now say "LIMPY BLINDY, thank you for saving me. LIMPY BLINDY, you'll go down in history." He never has to take his wooden leg off if he gets stuck in the mud, for the other animals now rush to help him.

It would be nice if children didn't behave like those naughty animals did at first and never called other people names, or mocked them because they were different in some way. After all, if Limpy Blindy hadn't been different, what would have happened to all those animals?

The Ballad of LIMPY BLINDY   by Ishbel Borland & Duncan Kennedy

The Ballad of LIMPY BLINDY

there's on - ly one thing to do".

TUNE 3

So he made him a patch and a wood-en leg so hecouldget a-

round,____ and just like all the oth - er lambs he loved to leap and

bound.____ He'd fro - lic and gam - bol in the fields and nev-er once com-

plain____ Well, hard - ly ev- er! Some__ times, aft- er a hea-vy

rain, he'd get stuck in the mud with his wood-en leg and have to take it

off.____ And all the oth - er an - i - mals would point at him and

The Ballad of LIMPY BLINDY

scoff.

(Spoken) : For sometimes animals can can be very cruel, just as children are who call people names. The animals would call out :

TUNE 4

"LIMP Y BLIND Y, wood en leg can hard ly see;

LIMP - Y BLIND - Y wood-en leg can hard-ly see."

TUNE 3

How - ev-er much they tea-sed him they'd nev-er make him

cry.——— He nev-er tried to get them back, he would-n't hurt a

fly.———And TUNE 1 then one sum-mer eve-ning (they talk a-bout it

yet) there was a dread-ful thun-der-storm which - no-one will for -

The Ballad of LIMPY BLINDY

The Ballad of LIMPY BLINDY

flames - their hearts were filled with dread.

They knew if no - one res - cued

them that soon they'd all be dead.

TUNE 3

But some-one's squeez-ing be - neath the door, good job he's ve-ry

small.____It's Limp-y Blind-y, brave lit-tle lamb, he's trying to save them

all._____ The farm-er had a wat - er tank just out-side the

door._____ It It had a wood-en spout he turned when - ever he washed the

The Ballad of LIMPY BLINDY

floor. Limp-y ran up to the wat-er keg as fast as he could with his

wood-en leg. He hit the spout a might-y clout, the spout fell off, the

wat-er rushed out. It poured all ov-er the burn-ing ground, the fire went out with a

HISSS!-ing sound. The farm - er was de-light-ed that Limp-y saved the

day, and res-cued all the a-ni-mals (plus fif-teen tons of

hay.) Now Limp-y goes a-bout the farm; he bears his name with

pride. The oth-er ani-mals bow to him and he feels warm in -

The Ballad of LIMPY BLINDY